FROM THE LIBRARY OF

Christina

The Best Figure Skater
in the Whole Wide World

This book is for the best daughters in the whole wide world — Tess and Lia — L.B.
To the Cote family — Stephanie, Michael, Jennifer, Suzanne and Marty — A. & L.D.

∽

Many thanks to A. J. Taillon and Frances Taillon for their fine
figure-skating advice and to Patty Cranston for her feedback and suggestions.

∽

Text © 2001 Linda Bailey
Illustrations © 2001 Alan and Lea Daniel

Kids Can Press acknowledges the financial support of the Ontario Arts Council, the Canada Council for the Arts
and the Government of Canada, through the BPIDP, for our publishing activity.

Published in Canada by
Kids Can Press Ltd.
29 Birch Avenue
Toronto, ON M4V 1E2

Published in the U.S. by
Kids Can Press Ltd.
2250 Military Road
Tonawanda, NY 14150

www.kidscanpress.com

The artwork in this book was rendered in mixed media, mainly gouache,
on Windsor & Newton cold-pressed watercolor paper.
The text is set in Minion.

Edited by Debbie Rogosin
Designed by Julia Naimska
Printed and bound in Hong Kong by Book Art Inc., Toronto

This book is smyth sewn casebound.

CM 01 0 9 8 7 6 5 4 3 2 1

National Library of Canada Cataloguing in Publication Data

Bailey, Linda, 1948–
The best figure skater in the whole wide world

ISBN 1-55074-879-3

I. Daniel, Alan, 1939– . II. Daniel, Lea. III. Title.

PS8553.A3644B47 2001   jC813'.54   C00-933348-7

PZ7.B34Be 2001

Kids Can Press is a Nelvana company

The Best Figure Skater in the Whole Wide World

Written by
Linda Bailey

Illustrated by
Alan and Lea Daniel

Kids Can Press

All Lizzy wanted was to be the best figure skater in the whole wide world.

When the World Championships came on TV, she watched every minute. Whatever the skaters did, Lizzy did the same. She twirled, she leaped, she spun around the living room floor. She lunged past the couch, and she lutzed around the lamp. It was the best feeling Lizzy had ever, ever had.

Her mom said she could take skating lessons at the community center. Lizzy couldn't wait. She tried her new skates on every night, turning them this way and that to make the blades twinkle in the light.

Finally, it was time for her first lesson. The teacher had blue skates with bells on them. She wore a twirly skirt like the world champions wore. Lizzy wanted a skirt like that. Desperately!

But skating on ice was a lot harder than skating on the floor. Lizzy's ankles bent in. Her toes got frozen. Her knees wobbled together. Again and again, she ended up flat on her bottom.

Her mom said it took a long time to become a world champion. She said you had to practice.

So that's what Lizzy did. She practiced every move the teacher taught. Not the spread eagle or the flying camel or the death spiral. Those came later. But after a while, Lizzy *could* skate backwards — a little. She could do a bunny-hop — sort of. She could hold one leg out behind her — almost straight. And she didn't land on her bottom nearly as much.

Nobody in the class practiced as much as Lizzy. Nobody came as early, or stayed as late, or tried as hard. Nobody else knew — already, for certain, with all their hearts, right down to the tips of their frozen toes — that they wanted to be a world-champion figure skater.

One day Lizzy's teacher made an exciting announcement. The class was going to skate the story of Snow White and the Seven Dwarfs in the winter carnival.

Lizzy's heart thumped as the teacher read out the names of the children who would be the seven dwarfs. *I* can be a dwarf, thought Lizzy. I'd love to be a dwarf! A voice in her head said, *pick me.*

One by one, as the teacher called their names, the dwarfs skated to the side of the rink. The dwarfs were all short, Lizzy noticed. She, Lizzy, was tall. The teacher called seven names. None of them was "Lizzy."

The teacher said they would need a prince, too, and a witch. Lizzy's heart thumped harder. She could be a handsome prince. She could be a horribly wicked witch. *Pick me, pick me.*

The teacher said a name for the witch and a name for the prince. Neither of them was "Lizzy."

The last main part, the teacher told the class slowly — and the most difficult part of all — was Snow White.

Lizzy looked around. There were hardly any kids left unpicked. None of them had practiced as much as she had. None of them had tried as hard. She closed her eyes.

Pick me, pick me, pick me.

The teacher said a name.

It wasn't "Lizzy."

Lizzy shut her eyes really tight so the tears wouldn't sneak out. She pressed her lips together hard. Through a roar of sadness, she heard the teacher say what the rest of the children would be.

Trees.

"It's not fair, it's not fair," said Lizzy as she sobbed into her mother's lap that night.

"I know," said her mom.

"I *hate* trees," said Lizzy. "They're stiff and hard, and they don't move, and I hate them."

"I know," said her mom.

It was the worst feeling Lizzy had ever, ever had.

The skating class started to get ready for the carnival. Lizzy watched the Snow White girl carefully to see if she would maybe twist her ankle, just a little, and need someone to take her place. But the Snow White girl skated smoothly around the rink.

One day the costumes came. Snow White got a twirly white skirt, just like the world champions wore. Lizzy got a tree costume. It was brown and green and made of cardboard. It didn't twirl.

Finally, it was the day of the carnival. The stands around the rink filled with friends and relatives. Everyone waited, excited, for the show to begin.

The trees skated out first — five of them, with Lizzy at the end. They skated slowly around the rink in a tree parade. They held their arms straight, like branches. They kept their legs stiff, like tree trunks. When they got to the place where they were supposed to be a forest, they circled around slowly and stopped.

And then they stood there. The way trees do.

Stiff.

After that, the *real* story began. The dwarfs hopped and spun. The witch charged around in angry circles. The prince darted through the forest. Snow White, in her twirly white skirt, did split jumps and mazurkas.

The trees just stood.

Finally, after a long cold time, the play ended. Snow White and the dwarfs and the witch and the prince whirled and spun off the ice. Everyone clapped. It was time for the trees to skate off. This time Lizzy was first.

She led the way, beginning a long slow tree parade around the rink, the way the teacher had taught them. Her legs moved stiffly. Her arms stretched out straight.

Suddenly Lizzy couldn't bear it! Not a moment longer.

She stopped. She put her arms down. Behind her, the other trees stopped, too, banging into one another.

Lizzy just stood there. The audience got very quiet. Everyone watched and waited.

Suddenly Lizzy did — a bunny-hop!

The other trees looked confused. All except for one. That tree
looked Lizzy straight in the eye. Then *she* did a bunny-hop, too.

A moment later, another tree did a bunny-hop. Then another.
Suddenly the whole forest was bunny-hopping down the ice.

Lizzy did a waltz jump. So did the other trees. Lizzy did a toe-loop. The other trees did, too. With Lizzy in the lead, the trees did a spin and a spiral and a shoot-the-duck. The audience laughed and cheered. Nobody had ever expected to see such an exciting forest.

When the music ended, the trees were right where they were supposed to be — at the end of the rink. They all took a bow, just as they were supposed to, and skated off.

Lizzy's mom was waiting.

"I couldn't help it," said Lizzy.

Her mom swept her up in the air, skates and all. "Lizzy, my love, you were a fabulous tree! And if I had my choice of all the figure skaters in the whole wide world, do you know who I'd pick?"

"Me?" said Lizzy.

"You!" said her mom.

Lizzy wrapped her branches tightly around her mom's neck.

Maybe it wasn't the *best* feeling she had ever, ever had.

But it was very, *very* good.